THIS BOOK BELONGS TO

Keeyah · Haynes

LITTLE RED RIDING HOOD

Written by Helen Anderton

Illustrated by Stuart Lynch

make
believe
ideas

Reading together

This book is designed to be fun for children who are learning to read. The simple sentences avoid abbreviations and are written in the present tense. The big type also helps children with their word-shape recognition.

Take some time to discuss the story with your child. Here are some ways you can help your child take those first steps in reading:

❋ Encourage your child to look at the pictures and talk about what is happening in the story.

❋ Help your child to find familiar words.

❋ Ask your child to read and repeat each short sentence.

❋ Try using some of the following questions as you go along:
   • What do you think will happen next?
   • Do you like this character?
   • What kind of voice would this character have?

Sound out the words

Encourage your child to sound out the letters in any words he or she doesn't know. Look at the key words listed at the back of the book and see which of them your child can find on each page.

Reading activities

The **What happens next?** activity encourages your child to retell the story and point to the mixed-up pictures in the right order.

The **Rhyming words** activity takes six words from the story and asks your child to read and find other words that rhyme with them.

The **Key words** pages provide practice with common words used in the context of the book. Read the sentences with your child and encourage him or her to make up more sentences using the key words listed around the border.

A **Picture dictionary** page asks children to focus closely on nine words from the story. Encourage your child to look carefully at each word, cover it with his or her hand, write it on a separate piece of paper, and finally, check it!

Do not complete all the activities at once – doing one each time you read will ensure that your child continues to enjoy the story and the time you are spending together. Have fun!

Little Red Riding Hood is shy. She wears a red hood to hide her curls.

One day Little Red's
Granny is sick.

Mom packs some food
to take to Granny.

Little Red takes the basket.
She skips into the woods.

A wolf asks Little Red,
"Where are you going?"
"To Granny's cottage,"
she replies.

Wolf wants to EAT
Little Red Riding Hood.
He has a plan.

Wolf sneaks into Granny's cottage. He eats Granny!

Then he waits for Little Red.

Little Red says,
"Granny, your eyes look big!
And Granny, your ears look big!"

"Granny, your teeth look big!"
says Little Red.
"All the better for me to eat
you with!" roars Wolf.

Wolf swallows Little Red!

A woodsman sees the wolf.
He saves Granny and Little Red

Little Red Riding Hood is not shy now. She teaches wolves how to be good!

What happens next?

Some of the pictures from the story have been mixed up! Can you retell the story and point to each picture in the correct order?

Rhyming words

Read the words in the middle of each group and point to the other words that rhyme with them.

bed

red

cape

bread

ear

plan

sick

shy

quick

thick

gate

hood

stood

good

wolf

bell

little

plan

man

ran

feet

good

eat

sweet

teeth

curls

dig

big

eye

pig

ow choose a word and make up a rhyming chant!

The **big pig** likes to **dig!**

Key words

These sentences use common words to describe the story. Read the sentences and then make up new sentences for the other words in the border.

Little Red does not **like** her curls.

Granny gets **very** sick.

Little Red goes to **see** her Granny.

Wolf has **a** plan.

He eats poor Grann

like · very · not

· are · but · help · with · all · we · can · his · up · ha

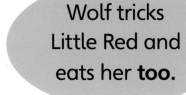

Wolf tricks Little Red and eats her **too.**

A woodsman comes to **help.**

The woodsman saves Little Red and **her** Granny.

Little Red is **not** shy now.

She teaches wolves how **to** be good.

the · and · a · to · see · in · he · I · of · it · too · you · they · on · she · is · for · at

ny · her · when · there · out · this · have · so · be ·

Picture dictionary

Look carefully at the pictures and the words.
Now cover the words, one at a time.
Can you remember how to write them?

cottage   curls   food

granny   hood   teeth

wolf   woods   woodsman